The Wizard of

A Play

Alfred Bradley

From the story by
L. Frank Baum

Samuel French - London
New York - Toronto - Hollywood

ISBN 0 573 05058 9

Please see page iv for further copyright information.

CHARACTERS

Dorothy
The Scarecrow
The Tinman
The Cowardly Lion
Aunt Em
Uncle Henry
The Good Witch of the North
The Guardian of the Gates
The Wizard of Oz
The Queen of the Fieldmice
The Wicked Witch of the West
The Witch's Cat
Glinda, the Good Witch of the South

Dorothy, the Scarecrow, the Tinman and the Cowardly
Lion go all through the play. All the other parts may be
doubled so that it is possible to stage the play with nine
players if necessary

COPYRIGHT INFORMATION

(See also page ii)

AUTHOR'S NOTES

In adapting L. Frank Baum's classic children's novel for the theatre, I have simplified the plot and also enlarged the character of the Witch to balance the forces of good and evil without which a series of adventures tends to amble along with little dramatic tension. The fact that the original story is set in Kansas has been ignored as the characters don't belong to any particular country and for many actors an American accent is not easy to come by.

This version of the play can be produced very simply, it needs no stage and may be performed in the round on the floor of a school hall. There is, of course, nothing to prevent a more ambitious production using back-projection, flash-boxes and all of the other magic which a proscenium theatre can provide but it is essential to keep the settings simple; this is the story of a journey and heavy sets of the Victorian toy-theatre sort will tend to hold up the action. It is useful to have the playing area broken up into a number of different levels and if these are planned to serve as the stile, the Witch's stove and the Wizard's chest, scene shifting will be cut to a minimum. If the rostra are painted in a neutral colour, lighting changes will produce strong contrasts which will add interest to the journey and imaginative use of light will provide the ditch and the river, and increase the effect of the Witch's spells.

With a simplified setting, sound becomes very important: some of the effects like the whirlwind will need to be pre-recorded but a percussionist equipped with a wide range of accessories will emphasize the fun of the Scarecrow's falls, help the actors to move from one scene to another and generally add to the excitement.

The costumes should present no difficulty but it is a good idea to prepare the Tin Woodman's suit well in advance so that it can be worn at rehearsals. Aunt Em and Uncle Henry are best dressed in grey or brown to contrast with the colourful world of Dorothy's imagination.

There are a number of points in the script where characters ask themselves questions and it is important, particularly at the beginning, to allow time for the audience to supply the answers so that they realize that they can join in. Dorothy starts it off when she is left alone after the disappearance of the Good Witch of the North and wonders aloud, "Now what did she say I had to wear?" If the convention is established early, the audience will give advice to the Scarecrow, hinder the Witch and warn the Tinman without having to be *asked* to participate. As yet, we have very few theatres which present plays for children regularly and it is not really surprising that actors coming across boldly drawn characters for the first time may be tempted to send them up: jokes about advertising, television personalities, politicians or local events may be all very well in a pantomime but they have no place in a play of this sort.

The Scatterbrained Scarecrow of Oz, a sequel to this play which takes Dorothy, the Scarecrow, the Tin Woodman and the Cowardly Lion through a completely new set of adventures, is also available from Samuel French Ltd. The same basic settings and costumes may be used for both plays.

ACT I

A farmyard with a fence and stile

Uncle Henry is whistling to himself as he sharpens a scythe. Dorothy climbs over the stile and runs across to him

Dorothy Hello, Uncle Henry.

Uncle Henry Hello, Dorothy. What have you been up to today?

Dorothy Oh, all sorts of things. We picked flowers in the wood and paddled in the stream, and we've walked miles.

Uncle Henry Who have you been with?

Dorothy Oh, just Toto. (*She takes her pet mouse from her pinafore pocket*) I expect he's hungry. I'll have to get him some cheese. (*She strokes him*) Isn't it peculiar, Uncle Henry, he understands everything I say.

Uncle Henry Does he?

Dorothy Yes, I'm sure he does.

Uncle Henry I wish *my* animals understood what I said to them, it would save me a lot of time.

Dorothy Perhaps they would if you talked to them as much as I talk to Toto.

Uncle Henry You'd best not let him out of your sight. There's been an old ginger cat as big as a lion hanging about outside.

Dorothy Oh! (*She pops Toto into her pocket, then realizes that her uncle has been teasing her*) Uncle Henry! You don't mean it?

Uncle Henry (*chuckling*) No, he's quite safe. (*He goes back to his scythe*)

Aunt Em (*off*) Henry!

Aunt Em enters

Uncle Henry Yes, Em?

Aunt Em (*as she comes in*) Have you put the animals away for the night? It looks like a storm brewing.

Dorothy Toto doesn't like storms. Do you?

Uncle Henry Nor do I. And I've seen my share. There have been some terrible storms not far away from here.

Aunt Em Do you remember that great storm? The sky was just like this.

Uncle Henry I'll never forget it.

Dorothy I can't remember.

Aunt Em It was long before you came to live with us child. When we first came here.

Uncle Henry It was more than just a storm; it was a cyclone.

Dorothy A cyclone?

Uncle Henry A mighty whirlwind that destroyed everything in its path; so powerful that it snapped great trees like twigs. That's why we made a cellar when we built this house—so that there would be somewhere to hide if another cyclone ever came.

Dorothy Can a wind really be as strong as that?

Aunt Em It's hard to believe, child, but there have been storms in these parts which lifted houses into the air and dropped them miles away.

Dorothy How terrible! (*Changing the subject*) Uncle Henry. Can I help you on the farm when I come back from school tomorrow?

Uncle Henry All right, I need somebody to lend a hand with the fence by the barn. And there's something else you can do.

Dorothy Yes?

Uncle Henry You can help me make a scarecrow.

Dorothy A scarecrow! I'd love that.

Aunt Em Henry! You'd better hurry. I don't like the look of that sky.

Uncle Henry I'll see to them now. (*He starts to go*)

Dorothy And I'll come with you. (*She peeps into her pocket*) Let's go and help Uncle Henry with the animals, Toto.

Dorothy and Uncle Henry go off

Aunt Em (*calling after them*) You'd better hurry, it's getting dark.

Aunt Em goes off

The sky gets darker. There is a crash of thunder and the sound of rushing wind

Aunt Em hurries back, calling. Uncle Henry and Dorothy follow her

Henry, Dorothy, come back. It's a cyclone coming! Quickly. Oh do hurry! (*She hurries into the house, opens the trap-door into the cellar and starts to go down*) Henry!

Uncle Henry (*buffeting against the wind*) Dorothy! Where are you?

Dorothy I'm over here!

Uncle Henry We must get to the cellar quickly. It's a whirlwind!

Dorothy I'm coming! You go in. I can't find Toto. He's hiding from the thunder.

Uncle Henry Don't worry about him. He'll look after himself. Hurry. (*He goes into the house and down the cellar*)

Dorothy Toto! Come on Toto, the thunder won't hurt you. I must find you! Oh, please come back. I can't go without you.

The wind rises to a crescendo, spinning her like a top

Toto! Toto!

There is a crash of thunder, and Dorothy can be heard calling Toto as she is carried further and further away. It is now pitch dark

A bird sings and when the Lights come back, the sky is blue and clear. Dorothy is lying on the ground where the wind dropped her. She slowly wakes up

Uncle Henry, Aunt Em, where are you? (*Calling*) Where are you? (*She looks in her pocket and finds that Toto is there*) Toto, there you are! Wherever are we? We must be a long way from home, I've never seen anywhere like this before. And I seem to have lost my shoes!

The Good Witch of the North appears

Good Witch You are welcome, most noble Sorceress, to the land of the Munchkins.

Dorothy (*getting up and dusting herself*) You are very kind.

Good Witch We are grateful to you for having killed the Wicked Witch of the East and for setting our people free from her spell.

Dorothy But there must be some mistake. I haven't killed anything.

Good Witch Well, your house did, and that is the same thing. See! There are the witch's shoes, still sticking out from underneath it.

Dorothy (*looking at them*) Oh dear. I'm very sorry. The house was blown away by a strong wind, a cyclone my Uncle Henry called it. It must have fallen on her. What shall we do?

Good Witch Nothing.

Dorothy Nothing?

Good Witch There is nothing we *can* do. She was wicked and she has paid for her wickedness. The Wicked Witch of the East we called her. She has held all the Munchkins under her spell for many years, making them slave for her night and day. Now that she is dead, they are all free and happy again.

Dorothy But who are the Munchkins?

Good Witch They are the people who live in the land of the East where the Wicked Witch ruled.

Dorothy Are you a Munchkin?

Good Witch No, but I am their friend. When they saw that the Witch of the East was dead the Munchkins sent a messenger to tell me about it. I am the Witch of the North.

Dorothy Oh, dear! Are you a real witch?

Good Witch Yes, indeed, but I am a good witch and the people love me. I am not as powerful as the Wicked Witch was, or I should have set the people free myself.

Dorothy But I thought all witches were wicked.

Good Witch Oh, no. You are making a great mistake. There were four witches in the Land of Oz, and two of them, those who live in the North and South, are good witches. I know this is true because I am one myself. The two who lived in the East and West *were* wicked; but now you have killed one of them so there is only one wicked witch in the whole Land of Oz—the one who lives in the West.

Dorothy But, Aunt Em told me that the witches were all dead—years and years ago.

Good Witch Who is Aunt Em?

Dorothy She's my auntie.

Good Witch Is she a grown-up person?

Dorothy Oh, yes.

Good Witch Then that accounts for it. Grown-ups don't believe that there are any witches left; nor do they believe in magicians, nor sorceresses. They don't even believe in Wizards.

Dorothy Are there really wizards as well?

Good Witch Of course! Oz himself is the Great Wizard. He is more powerful than all the rest of us put together. He lives in the city of Emeralds. (*She points suddenly*) Look!

Dorothy What is it?

Good Witch The Wicked Witch has disappeared. There is nothing left of her but her silver shoes.

Dorothy Oh dear!

Good Witch She was so old, that she dried up quickly in the sun. That is the end of her. But the silver shoes shall be yours. They belong to *you* now and you must wear them from now on.

Dorothy (*taking them*) But they're beautiful!

Good Witch The Witch of the East was proud of those silver shoes and there is some magic charm connected with them.

Dorothy A charm?

Good Witch Yes, she would never let them out of her sight.

Dorothy It's very kind of you to give them to me. I am very anxious to get back to my aunt and uncle. I'm sure they will be worrying about me. Can you help me find my way?

Good Witch Well you could go to the East.

Dorothy Yes?

Good Witch Except that there is a great desert and nobody has ever crossed it. Or you could go to the South . . .

Dorothy Yes?

Good Witch But there's another great desert there. On the other hand, if you went to the West . . .

Dorothy Yes?

Good Witch More desert. Even my home in the North is bounded by the same great desert that surrounds this Land of Oz. I'm afraid, my dear, you will have to live with us.

Dorothy I don't want to seem ungrateful but I must go home. (*She begins to cry*)

Good Witch Wait. (*She concentrates as she works her spell*)
Ep-pe, pep-pe kay-kay!
Hil-lo, hol-lo, hel-lo!
Ziz-zy, zuz-zy, zik!
(*In a matter-of-fact voice*) Is your name Dorothy?

Dorothy Yes.

Good Witch Then you must go to the City of Emeralds and perhaps Oz will help you.

Dorothy Where is the City of Emeralds?

Good Witch It is exactly in the centre of the country, and is ruled by Oz, the Great Wizard I told you about.

Dorothy Is he a good man?

Good Witch He is a good Wizard. Whether he is a man or not I cannot tell because I have never seen him.

Dorothy But how do I get there?

Good Witch You must walk. It is a very long journey, through a country that is sometimes pleasant and sometimes dark and terrible. But you must not be afraid. I will use all the magic arts I know of to keep you from harm.

Dorothy Won't you come with me?

Good Witch No, I cannot do that, but I will give you my kiss. No-one will dare to injure a person who has been kissed by the Witch of the North. (*She kisses Dorothy lightly on the forehead*) You must find the way to the Emerald City by yourself, but you will find the road is paved with yellow bricks so you can't miss it. When you get to the Wizard of Oz don't be afraid of him. Tell him your story and ask him to help you. Now I have to leave you. Don't forget, look for the yellow-brick road!

The Good Witch of the North disappears in a flash of magic, which gives the Scarecrow a chance to take up his position

Dorothy I'm glad that the Good Witch will protect me. Now what did she say I had to wear? The silver shoes, that's right. I wonder if they will fit me? (*She puts them on*) Yes, they do. They're very comfortable. Now then, what was the road to the Emerald City made of? Yellow bricks. Come along Toto, we've got a long journey in front of us. Let's look for the yellow-brick road.

As she starts to walk, the Scarecrow puts his head on one side and winks at her. She sees him and stops. He does it again

Scarecrow Hello. Good day!

Dorothy Did you speak?

Scarecrow Yes, I did, how do you do?

Dorothy I'm pretty well, thank you. How do *you* do?

Scarecrow I don't do very well. It's not much fun being perched up here day and night just to scare the crows away. My arms are getting very stiff.

Dorothy Can't you bend them?

Scarecrow No. I've got a pole stuck through the sleeves of my coat.

Dorothy Oh, I'm very sorry.

Scarecrow That's all right. Do you think you could take it out?

Dorothy I can try. (*She does*)

The Scarecrow's arms drop to his side

Scarecrow That's a lot better, but my back's very stiff. There's another pole behind me stuck into the ground. Could you manage to lift me off it?

Dorothy I'm afraid you'll be too heavy for me to lift.

Scarecrow Oh no, I'm very light. I hardly weigh anything at all.

Dorothy All right.

She struggles for a moment: he jerks off the pole and flops to the ground

Oh dear, I hope you haven't hurt yourself.

Scarecrow (*as Dorothy sits him up*) No, I'm fine. I fall softly you know. (*He waves his arms loosely*) That's a lot better. Do you know I was beginning to think I was stuck up that pole for ever. I can't tell you how glad I am that you came along. What's your name?

Dorothy Dorothy.

Scarecrow Dorothy. That's a very nice name. Where are you going?

Dorothy I'm going to follow the yellow-brick road to the Emerald City and ask the Wizard of Oz to send me back home.

Scarecrow Where is the Emerald City?

Dorothy I was hoping you would know that.

Scarecrow Me? Oh, no, I don't know anything. You see I'm just stuffed full of straw, I haven't any brains at all.

Dorothy Oh, I'm very sorry.

Scarecrow That's all right. So you're going to ask the Wizard to get you back home?

Dorothy Yes.

Scarecrow If I go to the Emerald City with you, do you think the Wizard would give me some brains?

Dorothy I don't know, but come along if you like, I'll be pleased to have company. *Perhaps* the Wizard will be able to help you but even if he can't, you won't be any worse off than you are now.

Scarecrow That's true. You see, I don't mind my legs and arms and body being stuffed, because at least I can't get hurt. If anyone treads on my toes or even sticks a pin into me, it doesn't matter, because I can't feel it. Just pinch me. Go on!

Dorothy pinches him

There, you see!—But I don't want people to call me a fool, and if my head stays stuffed with straw instead of brains, how am I ever to know anything?

Dorothy I understand how you feel. If you come with me I'll ask the Wizard of Oz to do all he can for you.

Scarecrow Thank you. How do we get there?

Dorothy Walk.

Scarecrow Oh dear!

Dorothy What's the matter?

Scarecrow I'm used to standing, that's easy. But I don't know how to walk.

Dorothy You don't know how to walk?

Scarecrow I've never needed to before.

Dorothy Well, it's quite easy. You just move your legs one at a time.

Scarecrow I see. (*He does, still sitting*) I don't seem to be getting very far.

Dorothy You have to stand up first. Use your brains.

Scarecrow (*sadly*) I haven't got any.

Dorothy I'm sorry, I forgot. Here, let me help you.

She helps him to his feet

Scarecrow Thank you. Now what do I do?

Dorothy You just lift one leg and then the other.

Scarecrow Lift one leg. (*He lifts one leg, holding it stiffly in front of him*) And then the other. (*He jerks the other leg up and falls over in a heap*)

Dorothy No. Not both at the same time! Like this. (*She shows him*)

Scarecrow Oh, like that. Right! (*He begins to walk cautiously*) I can walk! I can walk! (*He falls over*) I'll soon get the hang of it. (*He tries again and is soon walking confidently*) Now, we'd better set off. What is the road to the Emerald City made of? (*He gives the audience a chance to tell him*)

Dorothy Yellow bricks, that's right.

Scarecrow Well, we'd better look for them. If I had some brains I'd make up a song to help us on our way.

Dorothy Never mind, Scarecrow.

Scarecrow What's that in your pocket?

Dorothy It's Toto, my pet mouse. (*She shows him*) You needn't be afraid he won't bite.

Scarecrow I'm not afraid of a little mouse. (*He strokes him*) There's only *one* thing in the world that I'm afraid of.

Dorothy What's that?

Scarecrow A lighted match.

Dorothy Look over there

Scarecrow What?

Dorothy It's the beginning of the yellow-brick road. Off we go!

Scarecrow Why is it called the yellow-brick road?

Dorothy Because it's a road made of yellow bricks.

Scarecrow (*admiringly*) You are clever. I'd never have thought of that.

The Scarecrow sets off strutting proudly on his new-found legs, with Dorothy following. The sky gradually changes to suggest a forest. When they have circled the stage, they stop

It's a long way.

Dorothy We don't seem to be getting anywhere.

Scarecrow I think it's very pleasant where we are. I don't know why you want to leave this beautiful place and go back home.

Dorothy You don't understand. Home is home.

Scarecrow (*baffled*) Oh, I see. Do you know, I only knew *one* thing until you came along and showed me how to walk.

Dorothy What was that?

Scarecrow How to make a scarecrow.

Dorothy How did you know that?

Scarecrow I saw the farmer making me.

Dorothy But you couldn't have done.

Scarecrow Yes. Luckily, when the farmer had made my head, the first thing he did was to paint my eyes so I was able to see what was going on. It was blue paint.

Dorothy Yes. I can see.

Scarecrow Then my ears. The farmer said, "They aren't straight, but never mind, they're ears just the same", which was true enough.

Dorothy What did he make next?

Scarecrow Next my nose, then my mouth; but I didn't speak, because at that time I didn't know what a mouth was for. I had the fun of watching him make my body and my arms and legs; and when he fixed my head on I felt very proud. "This fellow will scare the crows fast enough," said the farmer, "He looks just like a man." Then he carried me under his arm to the cornfield and set me up on a tall stick, where you found me all alone. I just stood all day like this.

He sticks his arms out suddenly; Dorothy ducks, just in time

Dorothy Poor Scarecrow. Were you very lonely?

Scarecrow Yes. Lots of birds flew into the field, but they went away again as soon as they saw me. Then one day an old crow came and perched on my shoulder and said "Caw, caw. Fancy that farmer thinking he could fool me in such a clumsy manner. Any crow can see you're only filled with straw." Then he hopped down at my feet and ate all the corn he wanted. The other birds seeing he came to no harm, flew down and ate the corn too, so in a short time there was a great flock of them all round me. I felt very sad about my failure but the old crow comforted me, saying, "If you had some brains in your head you'd be as good a man as anybody, and a better man than some." After the crows had eaten all the corn, I thought over what he had said and decided I would try to get some brains. Then you came along. You know the rest, and from what you say, I'm sure the Wizard will give me some brains as soon as we get to the Emerald City.

Dorothy I hope so, since you seem so keen to have them. Well, shall we go on?

Scarecrow Oh, yes. (*He dances along happily*) If this road goes in, it must come out. And as the Emerald City is at the end of the road, we must follow wherever it leads us.

Dorothy Anyone would know that.

Scarecrow Of course, that's why I know it. If it needed brains to figure it out, I wouldn't have said it.

Dorothy If you see a place where we can spend the night, will you tell me?

Scarecrow All right. (*He stops*) It's very soft just here, would you like to go to sleep?

Dorothy Yes, I'm very tired. We'll take it in turns. Will you wake me up when you're tired?

Scarecrow I never get tired. That's the beauty of having no brains—you don't have to give them a rest. I'll keep guard.

Dorothy All right. (*She yawns*) I'm so tired. Good-night, Scarecrow.

Scarecrow Good night, Dorothy. My word, hasn't she gone to sleep quickly? Now I'd better mount guard. I'll march ten paces to the left and then ten paces to the right. Now which is my left foot? This one? Is this my left? No, that one! That's my left. Right? (*He marches*) One, two, three, four, er five, now what comes after five? Seven that's it. Six, is it? Haven't I got a lot to learn. I'll start again . . .

He is startled by a groan from nearby

What's that?

It comes again

Dorothy. Wake up, Dorothy!
Dorothy (*waking*) Hello, Scarecrow. Have I been asleep very long?
Scarecrow No. Very short. Listen!

The groan again

Dorothy What is it? (*She gets to her feet*)
Scarecrow I don't know. But I don't like the sound of it.
Dorothy Look, somebody's coming!

> *The Tin Woodman creaks in very slowly. He is made completely of tin and wears a funnel for a hat. He holds an axe rigidly over one shoulder and moves and speaks with great difficulty*

Scarecrow Did you say something?
Tinman I was groaning, to attract your attention. I've been groaning for more than a year, but nobody has heard me before.
Dorothy What's the matter? What can we do to help?
Tinman Get an oil-can and oil my joints. They're rusted so badly that I can't use them. If I'm well oiled I shall soon be all right again. You'll find an oil-can on the shelf in my cottage.
Scarecrow Where?
Tinman In my cottage. It's only a few yards away. Just behind me.

> *Dorothy runs to get the oil-can*

The Scarecrow peers at the Tin Woodman

Scarecrow It must be funny to be made out of tin.
Tinman It's not very funny when it rains.

> *Dorothy comes back with the oil-can*

Dorothy Now, where are your joints?
Tinman Oil my neck first please.

Dorothy oils his neck

Dorothy How's that?
Tinman (*turning his head*) Much better. Now my arms.

She oils the joints in each arm

That's wonderful. I have been holding that axe in the air ever since I rusted over a year ago, and I'm glad to be able to put it down at last. Now if you will oil the joints of my legs, I shall be all right once again.

Dorothy oils his knees. He moves about, stiffly at first, then he smiles

Tinman I feel like a new man. (*He walks up and down swinging his arms*)

The Scarecrow copies him

That's better. I might have rusted up completely if you hadn't come along. You saved my life you know. How do you come to be here in the heart of the woods?

Scarecrow We're on our way to the Emerald City.

Dorothy To see the Wizard of Oz, and we decided to stop here for the night.

Tinman It was lucky for me that you decided to come this way. Why do you want to see the Wizard of Oz?

Dorothy I want him to help me to get back home.

Scarecrow And I want him to put a few brains into my head.

Tinman (*as an idea strikes him*) Do you suppose he could give me a heart?

Dorothy Why, I suppose so. It would be as easy as giving the Scarecrow brains.

Tinman That's true. Can I come with you to the Emerald City and ask Oz to help me?

Scarecrow Yes, of course you can. We'd be pleased wouldn't we, Dorothy?

Dorothy Yes.

Tinman Thank you. I'd better take my oil-can with me because if I should get caught in the rain, and rust again, I would need it badly. Do you know, I could see it on the shelf in my cottage and I was too rusty to reach up and get it.

Dorothy It can go in my basket, Tinman.

Tinman Thank you. (*He places the oil-can in the basket*)

Scarecrow Now if we're all ready all we have to do is follow the blue-slate road.

Dorothy Yellow-brick.

Scarecrow Oh, yes. That's it, yellow-brick.

They set off, the Tinman leading followed by Dorothy and the Scarecrow who sings happily to himself. They walk briskly downstage to the apron where the Tinman stops suddenly

Tinman Look out, there's a hole!

Dorothy Oh!

She stops suddenly about four feet R of the Tinman. The Scarecrow, some distance behind, strides down between them and is about to go over the edge when they grab an arm each and pull him back to safety

Tinman Why didn't you stop when I warned you?

Scarecrow I don't know. I suppose it's because my head's full of straw. I'm brainless. That's why I'm going to see Oz. Have you any brains?

Tinman No, my head is quite empty, but once I had brains and a heart as well, so having tried them both, I should rather have a heart.

Dorothy Have you always been made of tin?

Tinman Oh no. Once I was an ordinary man, until the Wicked Witch of the East came along and bewitched me. You see, I fell in love with a beautiful Munchkin girl. I loved her with all my heart, but she lived with an old woman who made her do all the housework and didn't want her to marry anybody. She bribed the Witch to get rid of me and one day, when I was chopping wood in the forest, she enchanted my axe. I swung it like this and cut my leg off. I couldn't be a woodcutter with only one leg, so I went to a tinsmith and he made a new one for me out of tin.

Scarecrow That must have made you feel better.

Tinman Yes, it did, but the Wicked Witch wouldn't be beaten, and she made the axe slip again and again. First I cut the other leg off and then my two arms, but the tinsmith made me new ones. Then she made the axe slip and cut my body in half and my head right off.

Dorothy How terrible.

Tinman Yes, I thought it was the end of me, but luckily the tinsmith happened to come along and he made me a new head and body so I could move around as well as ever. But alas, now I had no heart, so that I lost all my love for the Munchkin girl, and didn't care whether I married her or not. I decided to make the best of it and I was getting along quite well until I got caught in a thunderstorm and got rusted up. It was a terrible thing to happen, but during the year I stood there I had time to think and I realized that the greatest loss I had known was the loss of my heart. While I was in love I was the happiest man on earth; but no-one can love who hasn't got a heart and so that's why I want Oz to give me one. If he does I will go back to the Munchkin maiden and marry her.

Scarecrow All the same, I shall ask for brains instead of a heart; because a fool wouldn't know what to do with a heart if he had one.

Tinman I shall ask for a heart. Brains don't make you happy and happiness is the best thing in the world.

They walk on

Dorothy How long will it be before we are out of the forest?

Tinman I don't know. I've never been to the Emerald City. My father went there once when I was a boy, and he said it was a long and dangerous journey. But I'm not afraid as long as I have my oil-can.

Scarecrow And nothing can hurt me, and we can both look after Dorothy.

Tinman Dorothy bears the mark of the Good Witch's Kiss on her forehead and that will protect her from all harm.

Dorothy What about Toto? What will protect him?

Tinman Who's Toto?

Dorothy My little pet mouse. (*She shows him*)

Tinman *We* must look after him.

The Lion roars in the distance

Dorothy What's that?

Scarecrow It doesn't sound like anyone I know.

Tinman It sounds like a wild beast.

The Lion roars again

Scarecrow A very wild beast! Oh! What shall we do now?

The Lion bounds in, roars at the Scarecrow, dabs him with his paw and whirls him over. Then he leaps across to the Tinman, roars again and knocks him into a clattering heap. He moves threateningly towards Dorothy, who is holding Toto in her hand, and roars louder than ever

Dorothy (*frightened, but putting on a brave face*) Don't you dare to bite Toto!

The Lion stops. She pokes him in the chest

You ought to be ashamed of yourself, a big beast like you, to bite a poor little mouse.

Lion (*petulantly*) I didn't bite him.

Dorothy No, but you tried to. You're nothing but a big coward.

Lion (*blubbering*) Boo, hoo! I know I'm a coward, I've always known it. But how can I help it?

Dorothy I don't know, I'm sure. (*Admonishing*) To think of *you* striking a stuffed man, like the poor Scarecrow who can't defend himself.

Lion (*looking at him curiously*) Is he stuffed?

Dorothy Of course he's stuffed.

Lion I wondered why he went over so easily. It was astonishing to see him spin round like that. Is the other one stuffed as well?

Dorothy No, he's made of tin.

Lion That explains it. Do you know he nearly blunted my claws? Ooh! When they scratched against the tin it made a cold shiver run down my back. What is that little thing you're holding in your hand?

Dorothy It's Toto, he's my pet mouse.

Lion Is he made of tin, or is he stuffed?

Dorothy Neither. He's an animal like yourself.

Lion (*amused*) He's a funny animal. He seems very small now that I come to look closely at him. (*Sad again*) No-one would think of biting such a little thing except a coward like me.

Dorothy Well, you'd better apologize to him.

Lion I'm sorry, Toto.

Dorothy That's better. Now the others.

The Lion helps the Scarecrow to his feet

Lion Sorry, Mr Stuffing.

Scarecrow That's all right. Think nothing of it. (*They shake hands*) You can call me Scarecrow.

Lion Are you all right?

Scarecrow Oh, don't worry about me. It doesn't hurt when I fall over, I'm filled with straw, you see.

Lion I see. (*He turns to the Tinman*) Sorry Mr Shiny. Are you all right?

Tinman Just a bit scratched.

The Lion helps the Tinman up

I'm called the Tin Woodman, you can call me Tinman for short.

They shake hands

Lion Thank you.

Dorothy And my name's Dorothy. Now we're all friends. Why did you frighten us like that?

Lion Did I frighten you? I was much more frightened myself. I'm a terrible coward really.

Tinman A cowardly lion?

Lion Yes, it's hardly my fault. I was born a coward. It wouldn't matter very much, but you see they call the lion the King of Beasts so all the other animals in the forest expect me to be brave. (*Sadly*) They used to tease me about being afraid.

Tinman But that isn't right. You shouldn't be afraid.

Lion I know. (*He wipes away a tear with the tip of his tail*) It makes me very unhappy, but what can I do about it? As soon as there's any danger, my heart beats twenty to the dozen.

Tinman At least that proves you have a heart. I haven't.

Scarecrow Have you any brains?

Lion I suppose so. I've never looked to see.

Scarecrow I'm going to see the Wizard of Oz to ask him to give me some because my head is filled with straw.

Lion (*looking under the Scarecrow's hat*) So it is.

Tinman And I'm going to ask him to give me a heart.

Dorothy And I'm going to ask him to get Toto and me back home.

Lion Oh, do you think he could give me some courage?

Scarecrow Just as easily as he could give me brains.

Tinman Or give me a heart.

Dorothy Or send me home.

Lion Then, if you don't mind, I'll go with you. My life is simply unbearable without a bit of courage.

Tinman Cheer up, Lion. Most people are cowards sometimes. We'll all be pleased to have your company on the journey.

Dorothy (*to Scarecrow*) Now, do you remember how we get to Oz?

Scarecrow Yes. We follow the road made of red tiles.

Lion Red tiles?

Tinman No, not red tiles, yellow bricks!

Lion Why don't you think, Scarecrow?

Scarecrow (*happily*) Because I haven't got any brains. But I'll get some when I see the Wizard. (*To himself*) Follow the grey-stone road.

Lion Yellow-brick.

Scarecrow Yes, that's what I meant.

Tinman (*exasperated but not cross*) Ooooh! Right. Off we go. I'll lead the way because I can use my axe to cut down any trees that block our path.

Lion And I'll go next to frighten any wild animals away.

Scarecrow Then Dorothy and Toto. And I'll walk behind to see that nobody gets lost.

Tinman Make sure you don't get lost yourself.

Scarecrow If I do, I'll be there to *find* myself.

Dorothy, the Lion, the Scarecrow and the Tinman march out of sight. When they have gone, the Wicked Witch of the West hobbles in with her cat in attendance. She peers after the travellers through her crooked telescope, gives an evil cackle and goes back the way she came. Dorothy returns followed by the Tinman, the Scarecrow and the Lion

Dorothy I can't see the yellow-brick road any more.

Tinman There it is. It is all overgrown but it's there all right. This way.

Dorothy Yes, there it is!

Tinman Oh dear! (*He starts to cry*)

Lion What's the matter, Tinman?

Tinman I've trodden on a beetle. (*The tears come again and he is unable to say any more because his jaw has rusted up*)

Dorothy Tinman, you mustn't be upset. You didn't mean to tread on it.

Lion Why is he looking like that? Why doesn't he say anything?

Scarecrow (*grabbing the oil-can from Dorothy's basket*) I know. It's the tears. They've rusted his jaw so he can't move it. Wait a moment Tinman. (*He oils the Tinman's jaw*) Is that better?

Tinman Thank you, Scarecrow. (*He eases his jaw*) That will teach me a lesson. I must look where I step. If I tread on another insect I'm sure to cry again, and crying rusts my jaw, so that I can't speak.

Lion But it wasn't your fault if you didn't see the beetle.

Tinman That's easy to say if you have a heart. You people with hearts have something to guide you; but I have no heart and so I must be very careful. When Oz gives me one of course I needn't mind so much.

They go further along the road

Dorothy I'm very hungry.

Tinman Let's rest here for a while.

Dorothy sits down

Lion If you like, I will go into the forest and kill a deer. The Tinman can chop some wood for a fire to roast it, and then you will have a very good breakfast.

Tinman Don't! Please don't. I should certainly begin to cry if you killed an innocent deer and then my jaws would rust up again.

Lion Suit yourselves. I'll just have a look round.

The Lion goes off

Tinman Now, a few sticks and we'll soon have a fire.

Scarecrow Fire!

The Scarecrow rushes off

The Tinman snaps some twigs which Dorothy lights and they sit in the glow of the fire

Dorothy Can you see pictures in the fire, Tinman?

Tinman I used to be able to when I was a real man but not any more.

Dorothy I can see lots of things. There's my uncle's farmhouse, and there's the face of the horse who lived in the field by the barn.

Tinman Can you see anything else?

Dorothy Yes, there's a river and a waterfall and a great palace with spires and turrets all dancing in the flames.

Tinman Perhaps that's the palace where Oz lives.

Dorothy Yes, do you suppose we'll ever get there?

Tinman Of course we will.

Dorothy I don't think I would have been able to go on without all of you to look after me.

The Lion comes back looking well fed

Did you find anything to eat?

Lion (*looking guilty*) Oh, just a few roots and things. Where's the Scarecrow gone?

Scarecrow (*off, from a distance*) I'm over here!

Lion Well you'd better come back, you don't want to go too far and find yourself lost.

Scarecrow (*off*) I can't!

Lion Why, what's the matter?

The Scarecrow peeps in, he has gathered some nuts

Scarecrow I don't like the fire. My straw is very dry and it only needs a little spark to make an end of me.

Tinman It's dying down. (*He stamps it out*) There, it's safe now.

Scarecrow Are you sure? (*He comes in*)

Tinman Yes, it's out. Did you find anything to eat?

Scarecrow There weren't any berries but I found lots of nuts.

He gives them to Dorothy who feeds some to Toto

You look as if you've had a good supper, Lion.

Lion (*trying to look as if he had not*) Oh, just a few roots and things, you know.

Dorothy I'll keep the rest in case we get hungry later on. All right Toto?

(*She puts the nuts in her pocket*)

Lion He doesn't eat much, does he?

Dorothy Well, he's only little.

Scarecrow Can you see the road, Tinman?

Tinman Yes, there it is. Are we all ready?

Dorothy, the Tinman, Scarecrow and Lion go off refreshed. A moment later the Wicked Witch of the West appears with an evil chuckle

Wicked Witch So, you're going to find the Wizard of Oz are you? Well, make sure you don't get lost. Cat, come here. (*No answer*) Cat, come here!

The Cat comes in without any particular haste. He carries two books

What's the matter with you? Why don't you come when I call?

Cat I'm sleepy.

Wicked Witch (*aiming a blow*) Perhaps that will wake you up. Where's my
book of spells?

Cat Here you are, Mistress Witch of the West.

Wicked Witch (*taking it eagerly*) Good. (*She reads*) "Take three onions and
some garlic . . ." That's not what I want. It's a cookery book. I want my
book of spells!

Cat I thought you said book of smells. Is this the one?

Wicked Witch Of course it is! Now, let me see. Yes, here we are. "To make
a ditch." (*She performs a ritual and makes a "ditch"*) Now they'll never
get to the Land of Oz!

*The Wicked Witch and Cat go off, laughing. Almost immediately the
Scarecrow, Tinman, Lion and Dorothy return. They stop suddenly when
they see the "ditch"*

Scarecrow What have we stopped for?

Tinman It's a ditch.

Scarecrow Is it deep?

Tinman I can't see the bottom but it looks very deep and there are sharp
rocks on the way down.

Dorothy What shall we do?

Tinman I haven't the faintest idea.

Lion Nor have I. It makes me nervous just to look at it.

Scarecrow We cannot climb down this great ditch can we?

Lion No.

Scarecrow And we cannot fly across it?

Lion No.

Scarecrow Then we must stay where we are.

Lion I think I could jump over it, as long as I don't look down.

Scarecrow Then we're all right. We can hold on to your tail and you can
carry us over one at a time.

Lion (*plucking up courage*) Well, I'll try. Who's coming first?

Scarecrow I will. If you find that you can't make it, Dorothy will be killed
or the Tinman may get badly dented on the rocks. But I won't matter so
much because the fall wouldn't hurt me at all.

Lion Hold on then.

Scarecrow Right.

Lion Hold on tight. (*He springs across with the Scarecrow*)

Dorothy Hurrah!

The Lion jumps back

Lion Are you ready Dorothy?

Dorothy Yes. Hold on tight, Toto!

*The Lion clears the "ditch" with Dorothy. He does not notice that the
Scarecrow holds on to his tail when he returns for the Tinman*

Tinman I'm sorry I'm so heavy.

Lion That's all right. Here we go.

The Lion springs across with the Tinman

Tinman Thank you. That was a brave thing to do, Lion.
Lion Not really. I was very frightened. I couldn't have done it with my eyes open!

They are about to set off again when the Scarecrow calls them from the other side of the "ditch"

Dorothy Oh, Scarecrow!

The Lion jumps back and returns with the Scarecrow

Tinman What did you do that for?
Scarecrow I don't know really. I just enjoyed the ride.
Dorothy When do you think we'll get to the Land of Oz?
Tinman It can't be much further. Are you still tired?
Dorothy Just a little.
Tinman Well, walk on as far as you can and then when you get too sleepy, I'll carry you.
Scarecrow I hope I don't have to carry the Lion.

They set off again and come to a "poppy-field"

Lion I think we must be getting near the Emerald City.
Tinman We seem to have left the jungle behind. Look at all the flowers everywhere.
Scarecrow Aren't they pretty? Are they buttercups?
Lion Of course not, buttercups are yellow.
Scarecrow Oh! They're the only flowers I've heard of. The farmer had a cow called Buttercup, you see.
Lion These are poppies.
Scarecrow Are they?
Dorothy Aren't they beautiful?
Scarecrow I suppose so. When I have brains I shall probably like them more.
Lion I always did like flowers, they seem so helpless and frail. But there are none in the forest as bright as these. (*He yawns*) They do make you feel sleepy.
Dorothy (*stretching her arms*) Oh, I can't stop yawning.
Tinman It's the poppies making you feel tired. We must hurry to the yellow-brick road. Dorothy, Toto, don't fall asleep!

But they do

Lion (*sleepily*) Beautiful, beautiful poppies.
Scarecrow What's the matter with them all?
Tinman The scent of the poppies is so strong that it's making them sleepy. If we don't hurry them out of this field they'll never wake up again.
Scarecrow Look, Lion, you run on as fast as you can. You must get away from these flowers. The Tinman and I will be all right, they can't hurt *us*.
Tinman Hurry, Lion. We'll bring Dorothy.

The Lion dances off in a daze, circles the stage once or twice and collapses, sound asleep

Scarecrow We'll make a chair with our hands, and carry her.

They carry Dorothy between them

Tinman She should be all right here.

They put her down gently

Scarecrow What about the Lion?

Tinman There is nothing we can do for him. He is much too heavy to lift. (*Sadly*) We'll have to leave him there forever. Perhaps he will dream that he has found his courage at last.

Scarecrow I'm sorry. The Lion was a very good companion. I don't know what we'll do without him.

There is a squeak for help and a Fieldmouse rushes on. She darts from one place to the other, not knowing where to hide. The cause of the commotion is the Wicked Witch's Cat, who stalks after her

Cat Now, I've got you at last! (*He prepares to spring*)

The Tinman raises his axe and shouts

Tinman Oh no you haven't. (*He chases the Cat away*)

Cat You wait until the Wicked Witch of the West hears about this.

The Cat scurries off

Fieldmouse Oh, thank you! Thank you for saving my life.

Tinman Don't mention it. I haven't got a heart, you know, so I am careful to help anybody who needs a friend, even if it happens to be only a mouse.

Fieldmouse Only a mouse! Why, I am a queen—the Queen of all the Fieldmice!

Tinman I'm sorry, your majesty. (*He bows*)

Fieldmouse So you have done a great deed, as well as a brave one, in saving my life. Is there anything I can do to repay you?

Tinman Nothing that I can think of.

Scarecrow Oh yes there is; you can save our friend, the Lion, who is asleep in the poppy field.

Fieldmouse A Lion! He would eat us all up.

Scarecrow Not this one, he's a coward.

Fieldmouse Are you sure?

Scarecrow He says so himself, and he would never hurt anyone who is our friend. If you will help us to save him I promise that he will treat you with all kindness.

Fieldmouse Very well, we will trust you. But what do you want us to do?

Scarecrow Have you many subjects?

Fieldmouse (*peering into the audience*) Thousands.

Tinman Can they squeak?

Fieldmouse Of course.

Tinman Do you think that they might be able to wake the Lion up if they all squeaked together?

Fieldmouse I don't know, but we can try. Can't we?

The Lion stirs as the audience squeak: he jumps in his sleep and finally rolls away from the poppies to safety

Tinman Thank you very much. You have all been very kind.

Fieldmouse I am the one to be grateful. I can never repay you for saving my life. If ever you need our help again, come into the field and call with this whistle. (*She hands it to the Tinman*) We shall hear you and come to your assistance.

Tinman We will. Good-bye!

The Fieldmouse goes

Dorothy (*waking*) Oh, that was a wonderful sleep and I had such a beautiful dream! I dreamed that I was home again and there were flowers everywhere. (*She sees the Lion*) I wonder what he's dreaming about?

Lion (*after waving his legs in the air, yawning and stretching*) Where am I?

Scarecrow On the river bank.

Lion How did I get here?

Scarecrow It's a long story.

Tinman If you're both feeling well again, we'd better be on our way.

The Tinman, Scarecrow, Lion and Dorothy go off. The Wicked Witch and Cat enter

Wicked Witch Cat, come here! Can you see anything?

Cat Yes.

Wicked Witch Well, what can you see?

Cat Four travellers.

Wicked Witch Four more?

Cat No, they're the same ones.

Wicked Witch Impossible. Nobody could get over that ditch.

Cat Perhaps they're cleverer than you.

Wicked Witch Nobody is cleverer than me.

Cat Then perhaps they're stronger than you.

Wicked Witch Nobody is stronger than me. (*She stamps in anger*)

Cat Then why are they still on their way to see the Wizard?

Wicked Witch I don't know. But I'll stop them this time. I'll make a wider ditch and I'll fill it with water until it becomes a great river. (*She performs another ritual and makes a "river"*) Now we'll see who's cleverest. They won't get over that!

The Wicked Witch and Cat go. The Scarecrow, Tinman, Lion and Dorothy enter

Tinman Stop!

Lion What's the matter?

Tinman There's a great river.

Dorothy How are we going to cross it? It's very wide and there isn't a bridge.

Scarecrow Now all we've got to do is cross the river and we'll soon be at the Emerald City.

Dorothy But how are we going to do that? I can't see a bridge.

Lion Perhaps we could swim across.

Tinman The current is too strong. We'd all be washed away.

Scarecrow What about using this great tree? If the Tinman can chop it
down so that it falls to the other bank, we can walk across it.

Lion That's a very good idea, one would almost suspect you had brains in
your head instead of straw.

The Tinman "chops down the tree" and they watch it fall to the ground

Tinman There we are. Now who's going first?

Scarecrow I will because if I fall off into the river it won't hurt me.

Tinman It would make your straw all wet.

Scarecrow I don't mind that. I feel safer when I'm not too dry. (*He crosses
the "bridge" like a tightrope walker*)

Tinman Now you, Lion.

Lion (*nervously*) No, you go next.

Tinman All right. (*He goes across*) Come on, Lion!

Lion (*more nervously*) I think Dorothy should go next.

Dorothy You mustn't be afraid, Lion. You jumped over the ditch,
remember?

Lion Yes, but it wasn't very wide and I didn't have time to think how
frightened I was. You go next.

Dorothy Come on, Toto. It isn't as difficult as it seems. It's all right as long
as you don't look down. (*She gets to the other bank*)

Lion I'll close my eyes.

Tinman No! You'll never get across with your eyes shut. Keep them open
but don't look down.

Lion (*trying to be brave*) Here we go.

*The Lion walks half way looking straight ahead then can't resist glancing
down. He groans and wobbles dangerously from side to side and is about to fall
in when the Tinman reaches out and pulls him along the "tree" to safety*

Thank you, friend. That was very kind of you.

Dorothy Have you noticed what's happening?

Tinman Everything is getting greener.

Lion I think this must be the Land of Oz. It can't be far to the Emerald
City.

Scarecrow I can't see any signs of a city.

Tinman Who's this coming?

*The Guardian of the Gates enters and walks towards them. He is a small
man dressed in a green uniform. He has a green box slung over his shoulder*

Guardian What do you seek in the Emerald City?

Dorothy We have come to see the Great Oz.

Guardian It can't be true.

Tinman Why not?

Guardian It has been many years since anybody asked to see Oz.

Scarecrow Well, we're asking now.

Guardian Are you sure you know what you are doing? Oz is powerful and terrible. If you come on an idle or foolish errand and bother him whilst he is busy he might be angry and destroy you all in an instant.

Scarecrow But it isn't a foolish errand or an idle one.

Tinman It is very important.

Dorothy And we have been told that Oz is a good Wizard.

Guardian So he is and he rules the Emerald City wisely and well. But to those who are not honest, or who approach him from curiosity, he is most terrible.

Lion Oh dear.

Tinman What does he look like?

Guardian That is difficult to tell. You see, Oz is a great Wizard, and can take on any form he wishes. Some say he looks like a bird; and some say he looks like an elephant; and some say he looks like a cat. To others he appears as a beautiful fairy or any other form that pleases him. But who the real Oz is, when he is himself, no living person knows.

Dorothy That is very strange. But we must see him, or we shall have made our journey for nothing.

Guardian Few people have ever dared to ask to see him. But I am the Guardian of the Gates and since you demand to see the great Oz I must take you to his palace. Are you ready?

Dorothy Yes.

Guardian Then first you must put on the spectacles which are kept in this box.

Dorothy Why?

Guardian Because if you don't the brightness and glory of the Emerald City will blind you. Even those who live in the City must wear spectacles night and day. Oz decreed that it must be so and ordered that they should be locked on. (*He opens the box and puts spectacles on each in turn, including Toto. Then he "locks" them with a tiny key attached to a chain which he wears round his neck*)

Dorothy How do we get them off again?

Guardian I have the only key. When you have seen Oz and wish to leave the Emerald City, you must return to me and I will unlock them. Now if you wait here patiently for just ten minutes I will go to Oz and tell him you are here.

The Guardian of the Gates goes

Scarecrow You don't look well, Lion.

Lion Nor do you, Scarecrow. I think it must be the green glasses.

Scarecrow Just ten minutes, and then we shall see the Great Oz. Do you know, this is the moment I've been waiting for all my life. I think I'm going to get my brains at last.

Tinman And I, my heart.

Lion And I, my courage.

Dorothy And in ten minutes I shall know if I can go home again.

Scarecrow Doesn't ten minutes seem a long time? It's just like waiting for Christmas.

The Lights fade and—

the CURTAIN *falls*

ACT II

Dorothy, the Lion, Tinman and Scarecrow are still waiting

Scarecrow Surely ten minutes are up by now.

Tinman Yes. Here he comes.

The Guardian of the Gate enters

Dorothy Did you see the Great Oz?

Guardian Oh, no. I have *never* seen him. But I spoke to him as he sat behind his screen and gave him your message.

Scarecrow Oh, good.

Guardian At first he was angry and said I should send you back where you came from. Then he asked me what you looked like, and when I mentioned your silver shoes he was very interested. And he was even more interested when I told him that you bear the mark of the Good Witch's kiss. That was when he decided that he would grant you an audience. But you cannot see him together, each of you must enter his presence alone. Dorothy must stay here. The rest of you wait outside.

The Tinman, Lion and Scarecrow go

Dorothy hears music

Dorothy What is that?

Guardian That is the signal. You must wait here until the music ends and then approach the throne.

The Lights dim and when the music stops she is in the palace. The Lights come up to reveal Oz sitting on a green throne. He is dressed like a wizard with a pointed hat. He has a long white beard and looks important and wise

A cymbal clash

Oz I am Oz the Great and Terrible! Who are you and why do you seek me?

Dorothy I am Dorothy the Small and Meek. I have come to you for help.

Oz Where did you get the silver shoes you are wearing?

Dorothy I got them from the Wicked Witch of the East when my house fell on her and killed her.

Oz And where did you get that mark on your forehead?

Dorothy That is where the Good Witch of the North kissed me when she said good-bye and sent me to you.

Oz I see that you are telling the truth. Very well, what do you want me to do?

Dorothy Send me back home where my Aunt Em and Uncle Henry are. I don't like your country, even though it is so beautiful. And I am sure my Aunt Em will be very worried about my being away so long.

Oz Why should I do this for you?

Dorothy Because you are strong and I am weak; because you are a Great Wizard and I am only a helpless little girl.

Oz But you were strong enough to kill the Wicked Witch of the East.

Dorothy That was an accident. It just happened, I couldn't help it.

Oz Well, I will give you my answer. If you wish me to use my magic power to send you home again you must carry out a task for me first.

Dorothy What must I do?

Oz You must kill the Wicked Witch of the West.

Dorothy (*alarmed*) But I can't.

Oz Why not? You killed the Wicked Witch of the East. There is now only one Wicked Witch left in all the land; when you tell me she is dead I will send you back home—but not before.

Dorothy (*nearly in tears*) But I have never killed anything willingly and even if I wanted to, how could I kill the Wicked Witch? If you, who are great and terrible cannot kill her yourself, how do you expect me to do it?

Oz I do not know, but that is my answer. Until the Wicked Witch dies you will not see your uncle and aunt again. Remember that the witch is wicked—terribly wicked—and ought to be destroyed. Now go, and do not ask to see me again until you have performed your task.

Dorothy goes out

Oz pulls off his steeple hat and beard revealing that he is a little old man with a bald head and a wrinkled face

Now then, who's next? The Scarecrow, I think. This mask should do for him. (*He puts on the head of a clown which he gets from an ornate chest*) That's it.

There is a knock from outside

Enter!

The Scarecrow comes in and bows

A cymbal clash

I am Oz the Great and Terrible! Who are you and why do you seek me?

Scarecrow I am only a scarecrow stuffed with straw. I haven't got any brains so I have come to you hoping that you will put some brains into my head instead of straw.

Oz Why should I do this for you?

Scarecrow Because you are wise and powerful, and no-one else can help me.

Oz I never grant favours without some return, but this much I will promise. If you will kill the Wicked Witch of the West for me I will give you such brains that you will be the wisest man in all the Land of Oz. Now go, and don't come to me again until you have *earned* the brains you so greatly desire.

Scarecrow Very well.

The Scarecrow goes

Oz jumps off his throne, removes the mask and does a little jig

Oz That's got rid of him. A man of straw if ever I saw one. Now what will be the best disguise for the Tin Woodman? I'll put on a beast mask and frighten him.

Oz dons his new head and returns to the throne as the Tinman knocks on the door

(*In a deep, impressive voice*) Enter!

The Tinman comes in

A cymbal clash

I am Oz, the Great and Terrible!
Tinman (*unimpressed*) Hello.
Oz Who are you and why do you seek me?
Tinman I am a woodman, made of tin. I have no heart, and cannot love. I have come to ask you to give me one so that I may be as other men are.
Oz Why should I do this?
Tinman Because I ask it, and you alone can grant my request.
Oz If you desire a heart you must earn it.
Tinman How?
Oz By helping Dorothy to kill the Wicked Witch of the West. When the Witch is dead, come to me, and I will give you the biggest and kindest and most loving heart in all the Land of Oz. Now go!

The Tinman goes away sadly

Oz removes his mask

I haven't had so many visitors for years. There's just the Lion now, I think. I know what will keep him at a safe distance. (*He puts on a golden mask like the face of the sun and returns to his throne*) Come in!

The Lion approaches timidly

Why didn't you knock?
Lion I was too n-n-n-nervous.
Oz I am Oz, the Great and Terrible! Who are you and why do you seek me?
Lion I am a cowardly lion.
Oz Are you afraid of me?
Lion Yes, I'm afraid of everybody. I have come to beg that you will give me courage.
Oz Why do you need it?
Lion So that I may live up to my name as the King of Beasts.
Oz Why should *I* give it to you?
Lion Because of all Wizards you are the greatest, and you alone have the power to grant my request.
Oz Bring me proof that the Wicked Witch is dead, and I will give you courage. But so long as the Witch lives you must remain a coward.

Lion But without some courage, I won't be brave enough to kill her. Couldn't you *lend* me enough courage to destroy her?

Oz That I cannot do. You must complete the task before you receive your reward. Now go!

There is a roll of thunder and the Lights fade. When they come back the Wizard has gone and the throne has disappeared

Lion Dorothy! Tinman! Scarecrow! Come here, I'm frightened.

Dorothy, the Scarecrow and Tinman hurry in

Dorothy What's the matter, Lion?

Lion I don't like thunder.

It gets brighter

Oh, I feel better now.

Tinman Did you see Oz?

Lion Yes. His head was a great ball of fire, like the sun.

Scarecrow I thought he looked like a clown.

Tinman He appeared as a great beast to me.

Dorothy That's strange. To me he looked just like an ordinary Wizard.

Tinman Do you remember what the Guardian of the Gates told us? He said that Oz can take any form he wishes.

Scarecrow It seems a bit like showing off, to me.

Dorothy He said that he would not grant my wish until I had destroyed the Wicked Witch of the West.

Lion He said the same to me.

Tinman And me.

Scarecrow And me too.

Lion Then the only thing we can do is seek out the Witch and destroy her.

Dorothy But suppose we can't.

Lion Then I shall never have any courage.

Scarecrow And I shall never have any brains.

Tinman And I shall never have a heart.

Dorothy And I shall never see Uncle Henry and Aunt Em again. (*She begins to cry*)

Tinman Don't cry Dorothy or you'll make me cry too.

Dorothy (*wiping her eyes*) I suppose we must try to do as Oz says; but I'm sure I don't want to kill anybody, even to see Aunt Em again.

Lion I will go with you, but I won't be much use. I'm too much of a coward to kill a witch.

Scarecrow And I will go with you, but I won't be much help because I'm such a fool.

Tinman I haven't the heart to harm even a witch, but if you go I shall certainly go with you.

The Guardian of the Gates enters

Guardian If you are leaving the Emerald City, I will remove your spectacles. (*He "unlocks" them each in turn*)

Dorothy Thank you. Which road leads to the Wicked Witch of the West?
Guardian There is no road.
Lion No road?
Guardian Nobody ever wishes to go that way.
Dorothy Then how are we going to find her?
Guardian That will be easy. Once she knows that you are in her territory
she will find *you*, and make you all her slaves.
Scarecrow Perhaps she won't because we intend to destroy her.
Guardian Oh, that's different. No-one has ever destroyed her before. But
take care, for she is wicked and fierce, and may not *let* you destroy her.
Keep to the West, where the sun sets, and you cannot fail to find her.
Dorothy Thank you.
Guardian Good-bye. Remember, keep to the West.

The Guardian of the Gates goes off

Scarecrow (*to nobody in particular*) Isn't it funny? Nothing's green any
more.
Tinman Will you oil my joints, Lion, so that I'm ready for the journey?
Lion Of course, friend. (*He oils the Tinman's joints*)
Tinman That's fine.
Dorothy Some of your stuffing's coming out. (*She puts it right*) That's
better.
Scarecrow Thank you, Dorothy.
Lion Are we all ready? The sun's beginning to set. We ought to be on our
way before it gets too dark.
Tinman Don't be afraid, Lion. We'll look after you.
Scarecrow Now we must go towards the East where the sun sets. (*He starts
off in the wrong direction*)
Lion The West!
Scarecrow All right, if you say so.

*Dorothy, the Lion, Scarecrow and Tinman march off: their silhouettes are
seen crossing the sky, which turns deep orange*

It grows dark. Evil music is heard

*When the Lights come up again the Wicked Witch of the West is preparing
a spell*

Wicked Witch Spin, spin, spin my spell.
           Make the winds their secrets tell.
           Spin, spin, spin . . .
(*She calls suddenly*) Cat! Cat come here!

The Cat enters

Cat What is your wish, Mistress Witch of the West?
Wicked Witch (*mockingly*) "What is your wish, Mistress Witch of the
West?" My wish is that you bring me my telescope. I want to see what's
going on.
Cat Certainly. (*He starts to go*) Where is it?

Wicked Witch I don't know. That's why I'm asking you.
Cat Very well.

The Cat goes off

Wicked Witch To think that that cat is the only friend I have in the world.

The Cat returns with the telescope

Cat Here it is.
Wicked Witch (*grabbing it*) Ah! Now we shall see. (*She puts it to her left eye*) Wait a minute, I can't see anything.
Cat Well, you won't will you? That's your blind eye.
Wicked Witch So it is. Ah, that's better. What's this I see? The four strangers again! And they're coming from the Emerald City. There's only one thing left.
Cat What's that?
Wicked Witch You are to go after them immediately and then tear them to pieces.
Cat Aren't you going to make them your slaves?
Wicked Witch No. One is made of tin and one of straw; one is a girl and another a lion. None of them is fit to work, so you may tear them into small pieces.
Cat Very well.

The Cat slinks off

Wicked Witch And don't come back until they are all dead.

The Wicked Witch chuckles in an evil manner as the Lights fade. When the Lights come up again, to sunlight, the Tinman is chopping his way through the woods, followed by the Scarecrow. Dorothy is being carried by the Lion

Scarecrow That must be hard work, Tinman. I wish I could help you. Let me try. (*He takes the axe and gives it a swing. It carries him round in circles*)

The others duck just in time

I don't think I'm the right weight for it, I'm sorry.
Tinman That's all right. I can manage, I never get tired.
Lion I wish I could say the same. I think I'll have to rest. (*He puts Dorothy down and then sits on the ground*)
Scarecrow You can use me as a pillow if you like. (*He lies down*)

The Lion rests his head on the Scarecrow's chest

Tinman It will soon be night so you mustn't rest for long. Now, I'd better sharpen my axe. I wonder what happened to that wicked cat? Still, I needn't worry about that, the mice will tell me if the Cat comes near won't they?

The Cat steals in

The Tinman tries to follow the instructions of the audience as they tell him

*where the Cat is. Finally he sees it and gives chase. The others wake up and
join in but finally the Cat escapes*

   The Cat runs off

Lion I don't like that creature. It makes my mane stand on end.
Scarecrow I've seen lots of cats before, but never one who looked as wicked
   as that.
Tinman I don't think that's an ordinary cat. I think it must belong to the
   Wicked Witch of the West.
Dorothy Then she must know that we are here.
Tinman Yes, we must be on our guard. She's probably watching us from
   her castle.

The Lights go down on the travellers and come up on the Wicked Witch

Wicked Witch (*looking through her telescope*) Useless creature! Now I'll
   have to waste one of my precious spells to destroy them.

   The Cat comes back

Useless, stupid creature. I don't know why I keep you.
Cat It's easy to talk. There's not much a cat can do against a man with a
   mighty axe.
Wicked Witch You didn't put up much of a fight; I saw you from here.
   (*She swipes at him with her telescope*) Now, where's my magic cap? Ah,
   yes! (*She takes off her steeple hat and dons a golden cap. Standing on one
   leg she chants the spell*)
     Ep-pe, pep-pe, kay-kay!
     Hil-lo, hol-lo, hel-lo!
     Ziz-zy, zuz-zy, zik!

*A clash of cymbals followed by a mighty wind. The Wicked Witch cackles in
triumph as it lifts the Scarecrow into the air, when he is followed by the others,
her joy knows no bounds. They are whirled round and finally dropped on the
floor of her castle*

That's better. Welcome to my castle. (*She takes off the magic cap and
replaces it with a steeple hat*) Now, you are my prisoners!
Dorothy What are you going to do with us?
Wicked Witch I haven't decided yet. Destroy you probably.
Scarecrow You may be able to destroy *us* but you won't be able to harm
   Dorothy because she bears the mark of the Good Witch's kiss.
Tinman He's right. Dorothy is protected by the power of good and that is
   greater than the power of evil.
Wicked Witch Silence! Or I'll have you both dropped from the tower.
   Now, man of tin, stand over there.
Tinman And if I refuse?
Wicked Witch Then I shall make a spark jump from my fire and set the
   Scarecrow alight. (*She points to a spot*)

The Tinman goes to the spot reluctantly

Now, I shall draw a magic moonbeam round you.

She waves her arm and the Tinman finds himself trapped in a circle of light

This ring binds stronger than any prison. (*To the Lion*) Now you; are you willing to be harnessed to my chariot?
Lion I am not. (*He roars*)
Wicked Witch You don't fool me with your roaring. (*She roars*)

The Lion runs away

Another magic circle for you.

With a further wave of her arm she traps the Lion in another circle of light. She suddenly turns to the Scarecrow

Now you can entertain me. I want to see you dance.

The Scarecrow hesitates

Go on—or I'll make a spark jump out at you.

The Scarecrow starts to dance. Weird music

That's right. Faster! Faster! (*When he is exhausted she snaps her fingers*) That's enough. You can fetch and carry for me. And you—(*she turns to Dorothy*)—can be my maid. (*She moves to the door and turns back to them*) Remember, if you disobey my orders, the Scarecrow will suffer.

The Wicked Witch goes out, laughing to herself

Scarecrow If you want to try to escape don't worry about me. I don't expect I'll ever get any brains now so it doesn't really matter very much if a spark does light on me.

The Wicked Witch returns with an old black kettle

Wicked Witch Dorothy, you will polish that until I can see my face in it!
Scarecrow You wouldn't think she'd want to with a face like that.
Wicked Witch (*turning to the Scarecrow*) You can sweep all the floors and then you will scrub out the moat! (*To Dorothy, with meaning*) Don't forget to keep my fire burning brightly. (*She turns to the Lion*) Have you changed your mind yet?

The Lion shakes his head

Then you won't get anything to eat until you do. I am the Ruler of the Land of the West and I'm used to being obeyed. (*She sits in her chair and begins to drop off to sleep*)
Scarecrow A fine ruler she is. She couldn't rule a straight line.
Dorothy (*whispering*) Scarecrow, do you see those keys she carries on her belt?
Scarecrow Yes.
Dorothy They must be the keys to this castle. If we could get them, perhaps we could lock her up in her own dungeon.

Scarecrow I'll try. (*He creeps towards the Wicked Witch. Just as he is about to steal the keys, a sneeze comes upon him*) Ahhtishhoo!

Wicked Witch (*instantly alert*) What's that?

Scarecrow Hay fever, I think.

Wicked Witch You're up to something I'll be bound. I'll soon stop that. (*She waves her arms like a hypnotist*) You will all sleep until I wake you!

They all go to sleep instantly where they stand

Cat! Come here!

The Cat enters

Cat Yes, Highness?

Wicked Witch Do you see those shoes the girl is wearing?

Cat Yes, they're silver.

Wicked Witch They're more than that, they're magic.

Cat Magic?

Wicked Witch They hold a great power. They used to belong to the Wicked Witch of the East.

Cat Well?

Wicked Witch I want them.

Cat Why don't you just take them?

Wicked Witch I can't. I have no power while she is wearing them.

Cat Well, she never takes them off so how are you going to get them?

Wicked Witch I have a plan. I'll wake her up and make her wash the floor. When she is busy, I'll put two iron bars across her path. She'll trip over, the shoes will come off and I'll get them.

Cat But she isn't likely to trip over two great iron bars. She'll notice them.

Wicked Witch Not these; I've made them invisible to mortal eyes. Bring them to me.

Cat (*going*) Where are they?

Wicked Witch On the landing! Now we will see who has the most cunning.

The Cat goes and then returns

Cat Here you are. There's one. (*He hands over an invisible iron bar*) There's the other. (*He drops it on her toe*)

Wicked Witch Ooooh! You clumsy idiot. Get out of my sight!

The Cat goes

Now to get the magic shoes! After that I shall have the power to destroy them all. Now wake up! (*She clicks her fingers*)

Everybody wakes up

Scarecrow That's a funny business. I've never been to sleep before.

Wicked Witch Dorothy. I want you to wash the floor. There's a bucket of water outside.

Dorothy goes off

When Dorothy is out of sight, the Wicked Witch places the "bars" in position

Scarecrow What's she up to?

Wicked Witch (*cackling*) You'll soon find out.

Dorothy comes back with the bucket of water

That's right Dorothy.

Dorothy gets on her knees and starts to wash the floor

No, I want you to start over there.

Dorothy goes towards the spot that the Wicked Witch indicates, trips over the invisible iron bars and one of her shoes comes off

Ah ha! (*She grabs the shoe and puts it on quickly*) Now our powers are even!

Dorothy (*getting to her feet*) Give me back my shoe!

Wicked Witch I shall not. It's mine now.

Dorothy You wicked creature! You have no right to take my shoe from me.

Wicked Witch I shall keep it just the same, and some day I shall get the other one as well.

Dorothy You won't.

Dorothy picks up the bucket of water and throws it over the Wicked Witch, who gives a loud cry of fear

Wicked Witch Aaaah! See what you have done! In less than a minute I shall melt away.

Dorothy It's only a bucket of water.

Wicked Witch Didn't you know that water would destroy me?

Dorothy Of course not. How should I?

Wicked Witch Soon I shall be all melted and you will have the castle to yourself. I have been very wicked in my time, but I never thought a little girl like you would make an end of me. Aaaaah!

The Wicked Witch rushes out and her moan dies away in the distance. She leaves behind her umbrella and magic cap and shoe

Dorothy (*looking after her*) She's disappeared. She's really gone! (*She puts on her magic shoe*)

Scarecrow We're free again!

Dorothy And we've done what the Wizard asked. Now we can go back to the Emerald City and claim our reward.

Tinman There's still one little problem to be overcome.

Scarecrow What's that?

Tinman The Lion and me. We can't move.

Lion We're still inside the magic circles and we can't get out.

Dorothy There's a book of spells here. Perhaps one of them will break the charm. (*She looks inside*) Oh, that's no use. It's in a strange language.

Scarecrow I've got an idea. (*He gets the Wicked Witch's umbrella and cuts off the "moonbeams" so that they can escape*)

Tinman I sometimes wonder why you think you need brains, Scarecrow!

Lion We're free.

They join hands and dance in a ring

Hurrah!

Dorothy Now, how do we find our way back to the Emerald City?

Lion Suppose we call the Queen of the Fieldmice? She said she would help us. Have you got the whistle she gave you, Tinman?

Tinman Yes, it's here. (*He blows the silver whistle*)

The Queen of the Fieldmice appears

Fieldmouse What can I do for you, my friends?

Dorothy Can you show us the way to the Emerald City?

Fieldmouse Certainly, but it is a long way off. Why don't you use the Magic Cap that the Wicked Witch left behind?

Dorothy I didn't know it was magic. What do I have to do?

Fieldmouse There is a spell written inside it. Place the hat on your head, repeat the spell and the winds will carry you wherever you want to go.

Dorothy And they won't hurt us.

Fieldmouse Oh no, they must obey the wearer of the Cap. Good-bye!

The Fieldmouse scampers off

Tinman Here's the Magic Cap, Dorothy.

She reads the spell written inside, puts the cap on and chants

Dorothy Ep-pe, pep-pe, kay-kay!

Scarecrow What did you say?

Dorothy Hil-lo, hol-lo, hel-lo!

Scarecrow Hello!

Dorothy Ziz-zy, zuz-zy, zik!

There is a cymbal clash, the Lights die away. Then the sound of sweet music which becomes a breeze. When the Lights return all signs of the Wicked Witch's castle have disappeared and the four travellers are floating in the sky which gradually changes from blue to emerald as they approach the Palace of Oz. They come back to earth

Tinman Here we are.

Scarecrow That was a quick way out of our troubles.

Lion It's extraordinary how a wind can become so powerful that it will lift a great beast like me high into the air.

Scarecrow Did you enjoy the ride, Lion?

Lion Yes. But I'm glad to have my feet on the ground again.

Scarecrow I wonder what the Wizard will look like this time?

The air is filled with music as the Lights dim. When they come up, there is an empty throne, inside which the Wizard of Oz is hidden

Oz (*in a solemn voice which comes from nowhere*) I am Oz, the Great and Terrible. Why do you seek me?

Dorothy (*looking around*) Where are you?

Oz I am everywhere, but to the eyes of common mortals I am invisible. I will now seat myself upon my throne, so that you may speak with me.

The throne brightens

Dorothy We have come to claim the promise that you made.
Oz What promise?
Dorothy You promised to send Toto and me back home, when the Wicked Witch was destroyed.
Scarecrow And you promised to give me some brains.
Tinman And you promised to give me a heart.
Lion And you promised to give me courage.
Oz Is the Wicked Witch really destroyed?
Dorothy She is.
Oz How did you make an end of her?
Dorothy I threw a bucket of water over her and she melted.
Oz Dear me, how sudden! Well, I must have time to think it over. Come back tomorrow.
Tinman Tomorrow! You've had plenty of time to think it over already!
Scarecrow We shan't wait a day longer.
Dorothy You must keep your promises to us.
Lion We've no patience left. (*He roars very loudly*)

Suddenly the throne begins to tremble nervously

We've had enough! (*He bangs the seat of the throne with his clenched paw*)

The front of the throne bursts open and the Wizard falls out like a clown through a paper hoop. He is a small bald-headed man who looks very nervous

Tinman (*rushing forward and raising his axe*) Who are you?
Oz (*in a trembling voice*) I am Oz, the Great and Terrible, but don't strike me—please don't—and I'll do anything you ask me.
Dorothy I thought Oz was a great Wizard.
Scarecrow I thought Oz had the face of a clown.
Tinman And I thought Oz was a terrible beast!
Lion I thought Oz burned like the sun.
Oz (*meekly*) No, you are all wrong. I have been making believe.
Dorothy Making believe? Aren't you a great wizard?
Oz Hush, my dear. Don't speak so loud, or you will be overheard and I shall be ruined. I'm *supposed* to be a great wizard.
Dorothy And aren't you?
Oz Not a bit of it, my dear. I'm just a common man.
Scarecrow You're more than that. You're a fraud.
Oz Exactly so! I am a fraud.
Tinman But this is terrible. How shall I ever get my heart?
Lion Or I my courage?
Scarecrow (*crying and wiping his tears on his coat sleeve*) Or I my brains?
Oz My dear friends. What do these things matter? Think of me, and the terrible trouble I'm in at being found out.
Dorothy Doesn't anybody else know that you're a fraud?

Oz No-one knows it but you four—and myself. I have fooled everyone so long that I thought I would never be found out. It was a great mistake letting you into my Throne Room. Usually I refuse to see my subjects, and so they believe I am something terrible.

Tinman But I don't understand. If you're not a wizard how was it that you appeared to me as a great beast?

Oz I'm afraid that was just one of my tricks. I'll show you.

He goes off and returns immediately carrying two of the heads

You see, they were just masks. I could change heads as often as I wanted.

Scarecrow (*looking inside the head*) This hasn't got any brains either.

Dorothy But how did you make your voice come from nowhere?

Oz I am a ventriloquist.

Scarecrow What?

Oz I can throw my voice wherever I wish. Listen. (*He demonstrates*) I learned that trick in a circus where I used to work. One day when I went up in a great balloon to attract a crowd, a mighty wind sprang up and carried me here. Seeing me come out of the clouds, the people thought I was a great wizard.

Scarecrow So did we.

Oz I ordered them to build this place and I called it the Emerald City. To make the name fit better, I forced everybody to wear green spectacles so that everything looked green.

Scarecrow But isn't it?

Oz Only here in my Throne Room.

Lion Why did you hide from everybody?

Oz I was afraid.

Lion But who was there to be afraid of?

Oz The Witches. You see although I had no magical powers at all I soon found out that the Witches were *really* able to do wonderful things. The Witches of the East and West were terribly wicked; so you can imagine how pleased I was when I heard that your house had fallen on the Wicked Witch of the East. When you came to me I was willing to promise anything if you would only do away with the other one.

Tinman And now?

Oz And now, I am ashamed to say that I cannot keep my promises.

Dorothy I think you are a very bad man.

Oz Oh no, my dear; I'm really a very good man; but I must admit that I'm a very bad wizard.

Scarecrow Can't you give me any brains?

Oz You don't need them.

Scarecrow That may be true but I shall be very unhappy unless you give me some.

Oz Well, I'm not much of a magician, but if you come to me tomorrow morning I will stuff your head with brains. But you'll have to find out how to use them for yourself.

Scarecrow Oh, thank you. I'll find a way to use them.

Lion And how about my courage?

Oz You don't need courage. All you need is confidence in yourself.
Lion Maybe. But I'm scared just the same. I need something to make me forget that I'm afraid.
Oz Very well, I'll give you that sort of courage tomorrow.
Tinman How about my heart?
Oz I think you are wrong to want a heart. It only makes most people unhappy.
Tinman That must be a matter of opinion. For my part I will bear the unhappiness without a murmur if you will give me a heart.
Oz Very well. Come to me tomorrow and you shall have a heart. I've played the Wizard for so many years that I may as well continue the part a little longer.
Dorothy And how am I to get back home?
Oz I shall need a little time to think about that. In the meantime you shall all be treated as my guests. My people will obey your slightest wish. There is only one thing I ask in return for my help—such as it is. You must keep my secret. Do you agree?
Lion Yes, we agree.
Oz Then tomorrow I will see what I can do for you all. Good-bye.

Oz goes sadly away

Dorothy He's a Great and Terrible Fraud but you can't help feeling sorry for him.

The Lights fade. When they come up again it is the following day. The Wizard is alone, meddling with some apparatus on a small bench

Oz How can I help being a fraud when all these people ask me to do things that everybody knows *can't* be done? It will be easy to make the Scarecrow and the Tinman and the Lion happy because they think I can do anything. But it will take more than imagination to carry Dorothy back home. I don't know what to do. I wish I'd never gone up in the balloon in the first place. I don't think I was cut out to be a wizard. Now, is everything ready? Yes, I think so. The first one should be arriving any time now.

There is a knock on the door

Come in!

The Scarecrow enters

Scarecrow Good morning. I have come for my brains.
Oz Ah, yes. You're sure you want them?
Scarecrow Yes. Even though Dorothy says she likes me the way I am. I'm sure she'll think more of me when she hears the splendid new thoughts my brain is going to turn out.
Oz Sit down in that chair, please.

The Scarecrow sits on the throne. The Wizard searches on the bench

Scarecrow (*imitating*) I am Oz the Great and Terrible!

Oz What was that?

Scarecrow (*falling off the throne*) Nothing! I was just trying to think what it would be like to be a great wizard.

Oz (*coming to him*) Now sit up straight. That's right. Can I take your hat off?

Scarecrow Yes. You can take my head off as well if it makes it any easier.

Oz I don't think that will be necessary. (*He takes the hat off*)

Scarecrow What's that?

Oz It's a little cushion full of pins and needles. From now on you will be very clever. (*He puts the pin cushion on the Scarecrow's head and replaces his hat*)

Scarecrow Very sharp! I must go and show the others.

The Scarecrow dances off happily

Oz I wish it was as easy to satisfy everybody.

There is a knock

Come in!

The Tinman comes in

Tinman Good morning.

Oz You haven't changed your mind?

Tinman No. I can't do without a heart.

Oz Very well. But I shall have to open your chest, so I can put it in the right place. I hope it won't hurt you.

Tinman Oh no, I won't feel it at all.

Oz gets a pretty red heart made of silk from the bench

Oz Isn't it a beauty?

Tinman It is indeed. But is it a kind heart?

Oz Oh, very! (*He opens a small door in the Tinman's chest and puts the heart in place*) There, now you have a heart any man would be proud of.

Tinman I am very grateful to you, and shall never forget your kindness.

Oz Don't mention it.

There is a knock

Come in!

The Lion comes in

Lion Hello, Tinman. Hello, Wizard.

Tinman Hello, Lion. I've got my heart. Would you like to hear it beating?

Lion Yes that would be interesting. (*He listens*) It sounds a good strong one to me.

Tinman I'm off to show the others.

The Tinman goes

Oz Now, it was courage you wanted?

Lion That's right.

Oz I'll get some for you. (*He goes to the bench and returns with a bottle of bright green medicine*)

Lion What is it?

Oz Well, if it were inside you, it would be courage. You know of course that courage is always inside one; so that this cannot really be called courage until you have swallowed it. I advise you to drink it as soon as possible.

Lion Right. (*He takes a gulp; it is not very nice*) Ugh!

Oz Come on. All of it.

The Lion gulps it down

Lion There!

Oz How do you feel now?

Lion Full of courage!

The Lion bounds off to tell the others. There is a knock, and Dorothy comes in

Dorothy I have come . . .

Oz I know my dear and I'm just going! I've hit on a wonderful idea. Will you meet me at ten o'clock tomorrow morning in the market square? I don't want to make any promises but I think I've found a way to get you home!

The Lights fade on Dorothy's happy face. A clock chimes ten and when the sky brightens we are in the market square. The Tinman is talking to the Lion

Tinman How do you feel, Lion?

Lion Full of courage. And you?

Tinman In good heart. Did Dorothy tell you to come here?

Lion Yes. She said that the Wizard was going to meet her in the market square to show her how to get home.

Tinman Here she comes now, with the Scarecrow.

Dorothy and the Scarecrow enter

Dorothy Hello everybody. The Scarecrow has been showing me his new brains.

Scarecrow I have to keep taking them out and polishing them. I don't want them to get rusty.

Tinman Now, if only Dorothy can find a way of going back home we will all have our heart's desire. Did the Wizard tell you how he was going to get you there?

Dorothy No. He just told me to meet him here in the market place at ten o'clock.

Oz comes in, bearing two heavy weights

Oz Ah, here we are! I'm sorry I'm late but these weights turned out to be heavier than I expected.

Lion What are they for?

Oz Just be patient. Now Dorothy. I've been thinking hard. The first thing you have to do is cross the desert, and then it shouldn't be difficult to find your way home.

Dorothy How can I do that?

Oz Well, I'll tell you what I think. You see, when I came to this country it was in a big balloon. Now I've found a lot of balloons and filled them with a gas which is lighter than air. If we tie them all together, they will be strong enough to lift us into the sky and carry us across the desert.

Lion Can little things like balloons be strong enough to carry people in the sky?

Oz Yes, if there are enough of them. But we must have plenty otherwise we might come down in the desert.

Dorothy Are you going with me?

Oz Yes. I am tired of being a fraud. If I come back with you, perhaps I can get into a circus again. That is if you don't mind.

Dorothy I shall be pleased to have your company.

Oz Thank you. Now if you would each bring some balloons and hook them to these weights we can be off in no time.

The Lion, Scarecrow and Tinman go and come back with bundles of brightly coloured balloons on wires, which they hook on to the weights

That's right, bring as many as you can.

Scarecrow Aren't they pretty?

Lion I like this pink one. (*He prods it with his claw, it pops*) I'm sorry. (*He begins to cry*)

Scarecrow It's all right, Lion, there are plenty more!

Oz Now then. I have issued a proclamation. See. (*He hands it to the Tinman*)

Tinman (*reading*) "Know ye all that I am going on a visit to see another Wizard. While I am gone the Scarecrow will rule over you. I command you to obey him as you would me."

Scarecrow Well I never! Now I'll really have to use my brains.

Oz Now, we only have to let go of the weights and we'll be off. Come along, Dorothy.

She holds on to one of the weights and takes the bundle of balloons which Oz holds out to her

Dorothy It seems that the time has come to say good-bye friends. (*Suddenly*) Oh! Where's Toto? Has anybody seen him?

Tinman I haven't.

Lion Nor me.

Scarecrow Nor me.

Dorothy Oh where can he be? Toto!

In her anxiety she lets go of her weight and hands the balloons to Oz. He drops the weight he has been holding and the balloons start to lift him from the ground

Oz Oh dear! Come along, Dorothy! I can't hold all of these balloons on my own. Hurry up or they'll carry me away.

Dorothy I can't find Toto. I can't leave him behind!

Oz (*trying to keep himself on the ground*) You'll have to leave him. I can't hold the balloons down. I can't hold them. There's a great wind pulling me. (*He leaves the earth behind*)

Dorothy Come back! Oh, please come back.

Oz I can't, my dear. I would if I could. Good-bye. Good-bye.

And Oz has gone

All Good-bye!

They wave until he is out of sight. Then they realize that Dorothy is crying

Scarecrow (*putting his arm round her*) I'm sorry, Dorothy. I know how much you wanted to go home. Now that I am the ruler of Oz I will have to use my new brains to find a way for you.

Tinman Although he was a fraud, I should be ungrateful if I didn't weep a little to see Oz go away. (*He begins to cry*)

Scarecrow Be careful.

The Tinman seizes up

Quickly, the oil-can! (*He oils the Tinman*)

Lion Dorothy, now that I have found my courage, would you like to come back to the jungle with me? I could make you a beautiful lair, and I'd be able to protect you.

Dorothy (*holding back her tears bravely*) It's very kind of you, Lion, but I must try to go home.

Scarecrow Just a moment. I've got an idea.

The Scarecrow hurries off

Lion He'll wear his brains out in no time if he isn't careful.

The Scarecrow returns with a big book

Scarecrow Here we are!

Dorothy What is it?

Scarecrow It's a book of spells that I saw in the Throne Room. I thought it would come in useful. (*He turns the pages quickly*)

Tinman Why didn't the Wizard use it against the Witches?

Scarecrow I don't think he had the brains for it. Here we are! (*He reads*) "The Magic Cap—the wearer of the Magic Cap is allowed three wishes. Each time the cap is used the magic words must be repeated." What magic words?

Dorothy I remember.

Ep-pe, pep-pe, kay-kay!

Hil-lo, hol-lo, hel-lo!

Scarecrow Hello! I like that bit!

Dorothy Ziz-zy, zuz-zy, zik!

For a moment nothing happens, then there is a sound of sweet music

The Good Witch Glinda appears

Scarecrow I didn't think it was going to work!

Dorothy Who are you?

Glinda I am Glinda, the Good Witch of the South. What can I do for you my child?

Dorothy I have had so many wonderful adventures and made so many friends but my greatest wish now, is to get back home.

Glinda I can tell you how to do that. But you must give me the Golden Cap.

Dorothy Willingly! It's of no use to me any more, and when you have it you will be allowed three wishes. (*She gives the Golden Cap to Glinda*)

Glinda (*smiling*) I think I shall be able to make good use of them. (*To the Scarecrow*) What will you do when Dorothy has left us?

Scarecrow I will stay here, for Oz has made me the ruler of the Emerald City.

Glinda (*to the Tinman*) And what will become of you?

Tinman I would like to find the maiden I loved so long ago. Now that I have a heart again I want to see her so much.

Glinda By means of the Golden Cap I shall command the winds to take you to her. That will be my first wish. (*To the Lion*) And what would you like to do?

Lion Over the mountains and beyond the river lies a great forest. I think I should like to live my life happily there.

Glinda Then my second wish will be that you should be carried to your forest.

Scarecrow And your third?

Glinda I shall command Toto to come back where he belongs—in Dorothy's pinafore pocket.

Dorothy Thank you. You are very kind and you are as good as you are beautiful. But you have not yet told me how to get back home.

Glinda The silver shoes you are wearing will carry you over the desert. You only need to wish.

Dorothy If I had known about their magic power I could have gone home the very first day.

Scarecrow But then I should never have met you. I might have passed my whole life in the farmer's cornfield.

Tinman And I might have stood and rusted in the forest till the end of the world.

Lion And I should have stayed a coward forever, and no beast in all the forest would have had a good word to say for me.

Dorothy You're right. I'm glad I stayed. But now I *must* leave you all.

Glinda The silver shoes have wonderful powers. They can carry you to any place in the world in three steps. All you have to do is knock the heels together three times and command the shoes to carry you wherever you wish to go.

Dorothy If that is so, I will ask them to carry me back home at once. (*She throws her arms round the Lion*) Good-bye, Lion.

Lion You won't forget me, will you?
Dorothy No, never. (*She hugs the Tinman*) Good-bye, Tinman. Now you mustn't cry, you know what it does to you.
Tinman Good-bye, Dorothy.
Dorothy (*kissing the Scarecrow*) Good-bye, Scarecrow. Think about me sometimes.
Scarecrow I will. Good-bye.
Dorothy Good-bye, everybody. (*She brushes away her tears and then clicks the heels of her shoes together three times*) Take me home to Aunt Em!

There is a rushing wind which spins everybody round. Dorothy is in the centre and the others move in a circle round her. As they spin faster and faster, they all drift off into the darkness until the little girl is left spinning alone in the centre. The wind dies with the Lights. When the sun rises Dorothy is lying in the garden. She gets up and rubs her eyes

I can't believe it. There's the barn and the fence and the farmyard. And there's the house. I'm home again. Aunt Em!
Aunt Em (*off*) Who is it?
Dorothy It's me, Dorothy!

Aunt Em hurries in

Aunt Em Dorothy! I don't believe it. Henry, come here quickly!

Uncle Henry hurries in

Uncle Henry What is it? Why, Dorothy! (*He hugs her*) I thought you were never coming back. Where have you been?
Dorothy Oh, Uncle Henry, I've had such a lot of adventures. The cyclone carried me away to a strange land where I met the most wonderful people. A Scarecrow and a Tinman and a Cowardly Lion.
Uncle Henry A Scarecrow you say, and a Lion?
Dorothy Yes, the Lion was a terrible coward. And the Tinman hadn't got a heart, you see. And we all went off to see the Wizard of Oz.
Aunt Em The Wizard of Oz. (*Smiling*) Whatever will you be dreaming up next, child!
Dorothy Oh, it wasn't a dream. (*She rushes on*) There was a wicked witch who made us her prisoners but she melted when I threw a bucket of water over her.
Uncle Henry The things you think of, child.
Dorothy I didn't just think of them Uncle Henry, they really happened!
Uncle Henry Well, I'll just put the animals away and then you can tell me all about it.

Uncle Henry goes off

Aunt Em And I'll get you a good hot bath ready. Welcome back, child.
Dorothy (*hugging her*) Oh, Aunt Em, I'm so pleased to be home!

Aunt Em goes off

Dorothy looks out at the audience

They didn't believe I had all those adventures. They think I've been dreaming but I know I wasn't. I'll never be able to make them believe me. *(She begins to have doubts)* Was I only dreaming? How can I be sure? *(She looks down)* Of course, my magic shoes! Now I *know* it wasn't a dream.

Dorothy dances away as the music comes up, and—

the CURTAIN *falls*

FURNITURE AND PROPERTY LIST

See AUTHOR'S NOTES

ACT I

On stage: Rostra
Fence
Stile
Twigs

Off stage: Scythe and sharpener (**Uncle Henry**)
Silver shoes (set in Black-out)
Basket for **Dorothy** (set in Black-out)
Oil-can (**Dorothy**)
Nuts (**Scarecrow**)
Book of spells, book of smells (**Cat**)

Personal: **Dorothy**: pet mouse
Tinman: axe
Wicked Witch of the West: crooked telescope, umbrella, keys on belt,
golden cap
Fieldmouse: silver whistle
Guardian of the Gates: green box containing coloured spectacles, key
on chain

ACT II

Off stage: Throne (set in Black-out)
Ornate chest. *In it:* ornate masks (set in Black-out)
Wicked Witch's chair (set in Black-out)
Crooked telescope (**Cat**)
Bucket of water (**Dorothy**)
Trick throne (set in Black-out—can be doubled with above)
Old black kettle (**Wicked Witch**)
2 ornate masks (**Oz**)
Bench. *On it:* pin-cushion, red silk heart, bottle of green medicine
(set in Black-out)
2 heavy weights (**Oz**)
Proclamation (**Oz**)
Bundles of balloons on wires (**Lion, Tinman, Scarecrow**)
Huge book of spells (**Scarecrow**)

LIGHTING PLOT

Property fittings required: nil
An open stage

ACT I
To open: General effect of full daylight

Cue 1	**Dorothy:** "A scarecrow! I'd love that!" *Start fade to storm*	(Page 2)
Cue 2	**Aunt Em** goes off *Darken sky further*	(Page 2)
Cue 3	**Dorothy:** "Toto! Toto!" *Fade to Black-out: pause, then fade up to sunlight*	(Page 2)
Cue 4	**Good Witch:** ". . . the yellow-brick road!" *Flash*	(Page 5)
Cue 5	**Scarecrow** and **Dorothy** walk round stage *Fade to dappled forest effect*	(Page 7)
Cue 6	**Dorothy** and **Others** set off on yellow-brick road *Fade up to full*	(Page 10)
Cue 7	**Dorothy** lights fire *Bring up red glow spot on* **Dorothy**	(Page 14)
Cue 8	As **Tinman** stamps out fire *Fade red glow*	(Page 15)
Cue 9	**Wicked Witch** performs "ditch" ritual *Bring up "ditch" shadow effect*	(Page 16)
Cue 10	**Scarecrow:** ". . . don't have to carry the Lion." *Cross-fade "ditch" effect to "poppy field"*	(Page 17)
Cue 11	**Dorothy** and **Others** exit *Fade "poppy field"*	(Page 19)
Cue 12	**Wicked Witch** performs "river" ritual *Bring up "flowing river" effect*	(Page 19)
Cue 13	**Guardian of the Gates** enters *Fade "river" effect*	(Page 20)
Cue 14	**Scarecrow:** ". . . like waiting for Christmas." *Fade to Black-out*	(Page 21)

ACT II

To open: As close of Act I

Cue 15   **Guardian of the Gates:** ". . . then approach the throne."   (Page 22)
             Fade to Black-out: pause, then bring up lighting on palace
                and throne

Cue 16   **Oz:** ". . . you receive your reward. Now go!"   (Page 25)
             Fade to Black-out: when throne and chest struck, bring up
                general lighting to half

Cue 17   **Lion:** "I don't like thunder."   (Page 25)
             Bring up lighting to full

Cue 18   **Dorothy:** "Some of your stuffing's coming out."   (Page 26)
             Fade to half

Cue 19   **Dorothy** and **Others** move off   (Page 26)
             Fade sky to deep orange, with characters in silhouette: then
                fade to Black-out. Fade up to sinister lighting when
                Wicked Witch *in position*

Cue 20   **Wicked Witch** chuckles   (Page 27)
             Fade to Black-out, then up to sunlight

Cue 21   **Tinman:** ". . . watching us from her castle."   (Page 28)
             Cross-fade to **Wicked Witch,** *retaining half light on* **Others**

Cue 22   **Wicked Witch** waves arm   (Page 29)
             Bring up spot on **Tinman**

Cue 23   **Wicked Witch** waves arm   (Page 29)
             Bring up spot on **Lion**

Cue 24   **Wicked Witch** exits   (Page 31)
             Revert to full lighting, retaining spots

Cue 25   **Scarecrow** holds up umbrella   (Page 31)
             Fade spots on **Tinman** *and* **Lion**

Cue 26   **Dorothy:** "Ziz-zy, zuz-zy, zik!"   (Page 32)
             Fade to Black-out, then up to sky effect—changing from blue
                to emerald

Cue 27   **Scarecrow:** ". . . will look like this time?"   (Page 32)
             Fade to Black-out: return to palace lighting when throne in
                position

Cue 28   **Oz:** ". . . so that you may speak with me."   (Page 33)
             Brighten lighting further on throne

Cue 29   **Dorothy:** ". . . can't help feeling sorry for him."   (Page 35)
             Fade to Black-out: return to previous lighting when bench in
                position

Cue 30   **Oz:** ". . . found a way to get you home."   (Page 37)
             Fade to Black-out: after clock chime, bring up market
                square lighting

Cue 31   **Dorothy:** "Take me home to Aunt Em!"   (Page 41)
             Gradual fade to Black-out: when set cleared and ready, fade
                up to full sunlight

EFFECTS PLOT

ACT I

Cue 1	**Aunt Em** exits *Thunder, wind*	(Page 2)
Cue 2	**Dorothy:** "I can't go without you." *Wind crescendo*	(Page 2)
Cue 3	**Dorothy:** "Toto! Toto!" *Thunder*	(Page 2)
Cue 4	As Lights come up to sunlight *Birdsong—fade as dialogue starts*	(Page 2)
Cue 5	**Tinman** "chops down tree" *Sound effect of tree falling*	(Page 20)

ACT II

Cue 6	**Tinman, Lion** and **Scarecrow** exit *Music: continue until Lights fade*	(Page 22)
Cue 7	Lights come up on palace *Cymbal clash*	(Page 22)
Cue 8	**Oz:** "That's it." *Door knock*	(Page 23)
Cue 9	**Scarecrow** enters *Cymbal crash*	(Page 23)
Cue 10	**Oz** puts on beast mask *Door knock*	(Page 24)
Cue 11	**Tinman** enters *Cymbal clash*	(Page 24)
Cue 12	**Oz:** ". . . you receive your reward. Now go!" *Thunder*	(Page 25)
Cue 13	As Lights fade *Evil music*	(Page 25)
Cue 14	**Wicked Witch:** "Ziz-zy, zuz-zy, zik!" *Cymbal clash followed by rushing wind*	(Page 26)
Cue 15	**Scarecrow** starts to dance *Weird music: fade as **Scarecrow** stops dancing, exhausted*	(Page 29)

Cue 16	**Dorothy:** "Ziz-zy, zuz-zy, zik!" *Cymbal clash followed by sweet music, which becomes a breeze—fade as Lights change to emerald*	(Page 32)
Cue 17	**Scarecrow:** ". . . look like this time?" *Music: fade as Lights come up*	(Page 32)
Cue 18	**Oz:** ". . . arriving any time now." *Door knock*	(Page 35)
Cue 19	**Oz:** ". . . easy to satisfy everybody." *Door knock*	(Page 36)
Cue 20	**Oz:** "Don't mention it." *Door knock*	(Page 36)
Cue 21	After **Lion** exits *Door knock*	(Page 37)
Cue 22	After Lights fade *Clock chimes ten*	(Page 37)
Cue 23	**Dorothy:** "Ziz-zy, zuz-zy, zik!" *Sweet music as* **Glinda** *appears*	(Page 39)
Cue 24	**Dorothy:** "Take me home to Aunt Em." *Rushing wind: continue until Lights fade*	(Page 41)
Cue 25	**Dorothy** dances away *Music until* CURTAIN *falls*	(Page 42)

MADE AND PRINTED IN GREAT BRITAIN BY
LATIMER TREND & COMPANY LTD PLYMOUTH

MADE IN ENGLAND